P9-AQD-468

# Junie B., First Grader
# Cheater Pants

*Look for all of these great books by Barbara Park*

**The Junie B. Jones series**

#1 *Junie B. Jones and the Stupid Smelly Bus*
#2 *Junie B. Jones and a Little Monkey Business*
#3 *Junie B. Jones and Her Big Fat Mouth*
#4 *Junie B. Jones and Some Sneaky Peeky Spying*
#5 *Junie B. Jones and the Yucky Blucky Fruitcake*
#6 *Junie B. Jones and That Meanie Jim's Birthday*
#7 *Junie B. Jones Loves Handsome Warren*
#8 *Junie B. Jones Has a Monster Under Her Bed*
#9 *Junie B. Jones Is Not a Crook*
#10 *Junie B. Jones Is a Party Animal*
#11 *Junie B. Jones Is a Beauty Shop Guy*
#12 *Junie B. Jones Smells Something Fishy*
#13 *Junie B. Jones Is (Almost) a Flower Girl*
#14 *Junie B. Jones and the Mushy Gushy Valentime*
#15 *Junie B. Jones Has a Peep in Her Pocket*
#16 *Junie B. Jones Is Captain Field Day*
#17 *Junie B. Jones Is a Graduation Girl*
#18 *Junie B., First Grader (at last!)*
#19 *Junie B., First Grader: Boss of Lunch*
#20 *Junie B., First Grader: Toothless Wonder*
#21 *Junie B., First Grader: Cheater Pants*

BARBARA PARK

# Junie B., First Grader
# Cheater Pants

illustrated by Denise Brunkus

SCHOLASTIC INC.
New York Toronto London Auckland Sydney
Mexico City New Delhi Hong Kong Buenos Aires

ISBN 0-439-57086-7

 Published by Scholastic Inc., 557 Broadway, New York, NY 10012, by arrangement with Random House Children's Books, a division of Random House, Inc.


12 11 10 9 8 7 6 5 4 3 2     4 5 6 7 8 9/0

Printed in the U.S.A.     23

First Scholastic printing, January 2004

# Contents

# 1

# A+ May

Monday

Dear first-grade journal,

Yesterday was the weekend.

The weekend is the ~~nikname~~ nickname of Saturday and Sunday. Only I don't know why.

Those two days zoomed by speedy quick. That's how come I didn't have time to do my homework. 'Cause what do I look

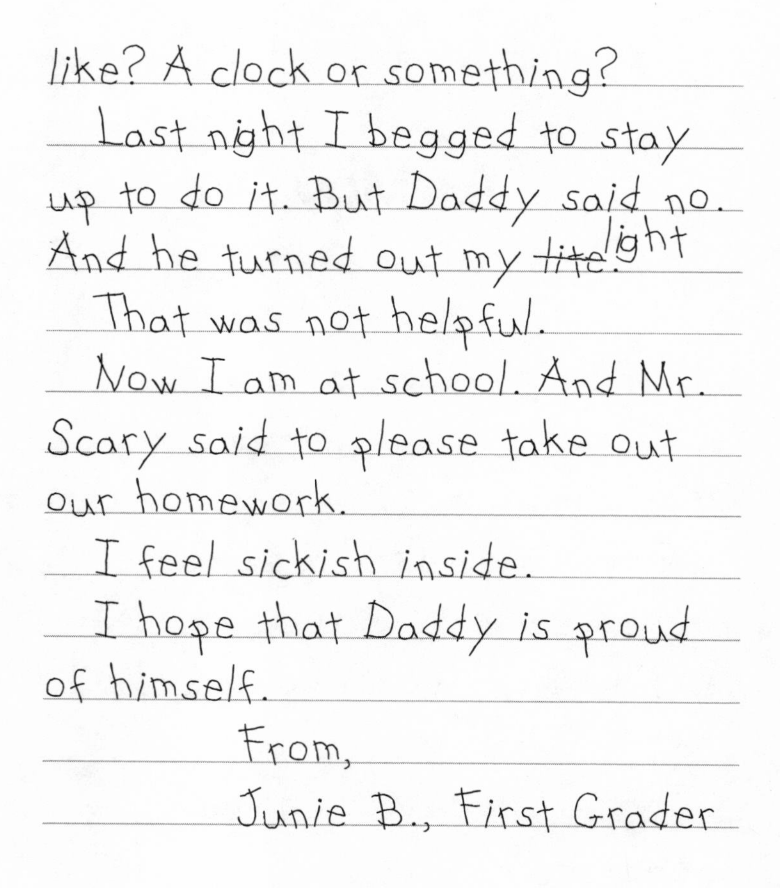
like? A clock or something?

Last night I begged to stay up to do it. But Daddy said no. And he turned out my ~~tite~~ light.

That was not helpful.

Now I am at school. And Mr. Scary said to please take out our homework.

I feel sickish inside.

I hope that Daddy is proud of himself.

From,
Junie B., First Grader

Next to me, May got her homework out of her backpack. And she put it on her desk.

She smoothed out her paper and smiled.

"I'm sure I'll get another A+ on this one. I get an A+ on *all* my homework papers, Junie Jones," she said. "One time, my homework was so perfect, Mr. Scary sent a happy note home to my mom and dad."

I did a shrug. "Blah, blah, blah," I said back.

May did a mad face at me.

Then she quick tapped Lennie on the back of his head.

"Lennie, did you hear what I just said to Junie Jones?" she asked. "I told her that I always, always get A+'s on my homework."

Lennie turned around.

"Please don't touch my hair, May," he said. "I used my brand-new gel to spike it today. And I don't want you messing it up."

I waved at Lennie across the aisle.

"I would *never* touch your hair, Leonard," I said. "Your hair looks like an interesting glob of artwork, almost. And artwork should just be gawked at."

Lennie nodded. "Thank you, Junie B. Jones."

"You're welcome, Lennie Whose-Last-Name-Starts-with-an-S, I think," I said.

After that, I smiled at May very smuggy.

Lennie likes me *way* better than he likes her.

May squinted her eyes at me. "How come you didn't take your homework out yet, Junie Jones?" she asked. "You're not following directions very well this morning, are you?"

I did a big breath.

Then I quick reached into my backpack. And I pulled out a rumpled paper. And I pretended it was my homework.

"There," I said. "There's my homework. Now please mind your own beeswax, you snoopy pooper, May."

May's face got reddish and flushy.

She started to raise her hand to tattletale. Only just then, the teacher called her name.

"May? It's your day to take the attendance sheet to the office," he said. "Would you like to come up here and get it, please?"

"Yes!" she said. "I would *love* to, Mr. Scary!"

The attendance sheet is when teachers send the names of the absent children to the office.

I do not actually approve of that practice.

May hurried to the front of the room.

"I'm *never* absent, Mr. Scary," she said. "I'm always, always here. Have you ever noticed that? Huh? Have you ever noticed how I'm always, always here?"

Mr. Scary closed his eyes for a second.

"Oh, yes, May," he said. "Believe me. I've noticed."

May did a giggle. "Also, I'm always punctual," she said. "Have you noticed that, too? Have you noticed how punctual I am?"

She smiled at the class.

"*Punctual* means 'on time,' everyone," she explained. "Last year, I was so punctual, I got the Punctual Award. The Punctual Award is an award for the child who is the most punctual."

Mr. Scary stared at her. He said to please stop saying *punctual.*

After that, May took the attendance sheet. And she skipped to the door.

"Don't worry, Room One. I will get this attendance sheet to the office all safe and sound," she said real loud. "Then everyone who isn't here will get reported to the principal. And that's *exactly* what they deserve."

Mr. Scary did a sigh. "Please, May. Just go, okay?" he said.

May did a wave. Then she hurried out the door.

After she was gone, I roamed my eyes around the room. All of the children had their homework papers out but me.

My insides felt sickish again. 'Cause pretty soon Mr. Scary would find out that I didn't do my assignment.

I swallowed real hard.

My eyes kept on roaming around.

And then what do you know? They roamed over to May's desk.

And surprise, surprise!

I saw her homework paper sitting there!

It was right out in plain view, I mean!

My heart pounded and pounded at that sight. 'Cause my brain was getting an idea, that's why.

I tapped on my chin very thinking.

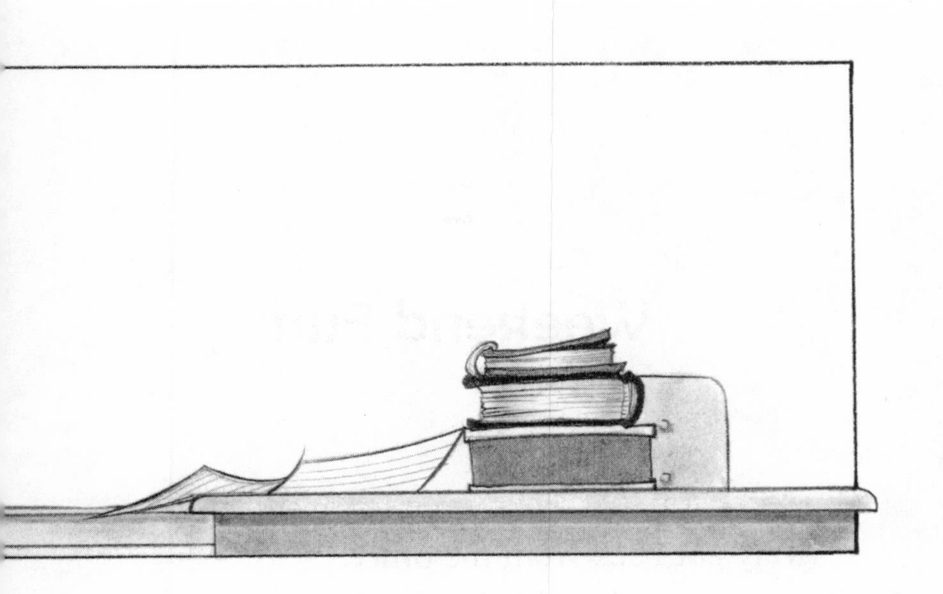

Then, quiet as a mouse, I pulled May's paper a little closer. And I copied what it said.

After I got done, I breathed in relief.

'Cause now I had a homework paper!

I smiled to just myself.

Then I closed my eyes.

And I whispered *thank you* to May for letting me borrow her homework.

# 2

# Weekend Fun

May got back from the office.

She stood at the door and waved again.

"I did it, everyone! I got the attendance sheet to the office. Just like I promised."

She looked at Mr. Scary. "It went very well, too," she said. "There were no problems I couldn't handle."

Mr. Scary raised his eyes from what he was doing.

"Okay . . . well, thank you, May. You can take your seat now, please," he said.

But May kept right on talking.

"At first, I didn't know where to put it. But then the secretary told me to put it in the wire basket. So I followed her directions perfectly," she said.

Mr. Scary pointed at her seat. "Excellent," he said. "Now please sit down, okay?"

May didn't pay attention again.

"When I was in kindergarten, I got an E+ for following directions," she said. "E+ is better than excellent. The plus sign means extra, *extra* excellent."

Just then, Mr. Scary stood up. And he took May's hand. And he walked her to her seat.

As soon as he went back to his desk, I strained my brain for something nice to say to her. 'Cause I was still happy at May for leaving her homework out.

Finally, I tapped on her arm. And I smiled.

"Welcome back, madam," I said real friendly.

May did a frown at me. "What kind of crack was *that*?" she said.

I just looked at her.

Friendly does not come natural to us, I think.

Pretty soon, Mr. Scary stood up at his desk. Then he walked to the board and he wrote these words:

*This weekend, one thing I did for fun was . . .*

"Okay, everyone," he said. "For your homework over the weekend, I asked you to complete that sentence, remember?"

Room One nodded.

"Good," said Mr. Scary. "Because this

morning, I'd like for each of you to read your homework paper to the class. That way we'll find out what our classmates do for enjoyment. Doesn't that sound fun?"

Room One nodded again. Even if it doesn't sound fun, you still have to nod.

Mr. Scary smiled. "We'll go up and

down each row until everyone gets a turn."

He pointed at Lucille. "Lucille, why don't you start us off?" he said.

Lucille sits in the first row by the window. Last year, me and her were bestest friends. But this year, we're just regular.

Lucille stood up and fluffed herself. Then she picked up her paper. And she started to read.

"This weekend, one thing I did for fun was . . . my richie nanna took me to her expensive beauty salon. And both of us got manicures and pedicures."

Mr. Scary looked surprised at that news.

"You got a pedicure, Lucille? Wow! That's pretty fancy stuff, isn't it?" he said.

Lucille shrugged. "For some people, maybe," she said.

She looked down and kept on reading.

"Also, we each got a papaya-fruit facial. And Nanna got an herbal body wrap. Plus I got a seaweed scalp massage."

Mr. Scary stood there for a second. Then he nodded very slow.

"All rightie, then," he said.

After that, he pointed to Camille.

Camille is the sister of Chenille. Those two are twin sets.

Camille stood up. "This weekend, Chenille and I made a puppet theater out of a cardboard box. And we put on a show for our little brother, Neil."

Mr. Scary beamed at that news.

"Oh, that's *great,* girls," he said. "I bet doing a puppet show for your brother was a lot of fun, wasn't it?"

"Not really," said Camille. "Neil kept on grabbing the puppets off our hands. And he made them kill each other."

"We don't like Neil," said Chenille.

"Neil is a boob," said Camille.

Mr. Scary just stood there some more.

Then finally, he moved on to Roger.

Roger was the best one so far.

"This weekend, one thing I did for fun was . . . I went to get pizza with my dad. And I ate a whole entire *anchovy*! And I didn't throw up till I was almost home!"

Room One clapped and clapped for that amazing story.

Mr. Scary was right.

It *was* fun to learn what our classmates did on the weekend.

I couldn't wait for it to be my turn. 'Cause I love to talk in front of the class, of course. Plus all I had to do was tell about my weekend, and Mr. Scary would think I did my homework!

I put the paper I copied from May into my desk.

I didn't need it after all.

'Cause what do you know?

Today I lucked out!

# 3

# Twitching

Finally, we got to the row right next to mine.

That is where José and Lennie sit.

When José's turn came, he smiled very proud.

He said on Saturday his daddy bought him brand-new soccer shoes. And he wore them to his soccer game. And he kicked the winning goalie with those things!

Lennie went next.

He said he got brand-new hair gel. Plus also, he got a thickening cream.

"A thickening cream can make even the thinnest hair feel rich and full," he said.

"Whoa," I said.

"Whoa," said Herb and José.

*Whoa* is what we say to be supportive.

May sits behind Lennie.

She stood up. And she read her paper real loud.

"This weekend, one thing I did for fun was . . . on Saturday, I made a pot in my pottery class. And after that, I was punctual to my ballet class. And the teacher said I danced like a *gazelle*!"

Mr. Scary did a chuckle. "A gazelle, huh?" he said. "A gazelle is a very graceful animal, isn't it?"

"Yes," said May. "Would you like to see me do a few steps?"

After that, she ran to the front of the

room. And she started to ballet. But Mr. Scary said to please sit down again.

As soon as she got back, I jumped right up.

"My turn! My turn!" I said real thrilled.

I tapped on my chin. "Okay, well, let's see now . . . on Saturday my grampa Frank Miller came to baby-sit me. And he let me roller-skate in the house. Plus also, he let me jump on Mother's bouncy bed. Only pretty soon, I got very pooped. And so I ran into the kitchen. And I drank chocolate milk right out of the *carton.* Without even a *glass,* I mean!"

"Whoa!" said Herb.

"Whoa!" said Lennie and José.

Mr. Scary raised his hand to interrupt me.

"Uh . . . excuse me, Junie B.," he said.

"It sounds like you had a great time on Saturday. But I'm wondering why you're not reading from your homework paper."

Just then, my heart got poundy and nervous. 'Cause I should have thought about that problem.

I swallowed real hard. "Um, uh . . . . well, let's see," I said kind of quiet. "Why aren't I reading?"

Mr. Scary smiled. "It's all right," he said. "You can start over. Just take out your paper and read us what you wrote."

After that, I stood there very frozen. And I couldn't even move.

Mr. Scary crossed his arms at me.

"You *do* have a homework paper, don't you, Junie B.?" he asked next.

I stood there a little while longer.

Then finally, I reached into my desk.

And I pulled out the homework I copied from May.

I waved it in the air kind of weakish.

"Here it is," I said. "Here's my homework paper. See it? It's right here."

Mr. Scary nodded. "Yes. Good. Now could you read it for us, please?" he asked.

I took a deep breath.

Then I looked down at my paper.

And I read it silently . . . to just myself.

"Okay. Done," I said.

After that, I quick sat down. And I stuffed the paper back into my desk.

Mr. Scary came back to where I sit.

He said could he please see my paper?

I felt shaky and sickish inside.

Very slow, I took out my paper again. And I handed it over.

After he read it, he shook his head.

Then he took my hand. And he walked me into the hall.

"It seems that you and May had *very* similar weekends. Doesn't it, Junie B.?" he said.

I did a gulp. "Yes," I said. "It does."

Mr. Scary read my paper once more.

"So . . . you take a pottery class, do you?" he said.

I rocked back and forth on my feet.

"Yup, yup. I do," I said. "I take a pottery class. And I make little . . . well, you know . . . pots."

Mr. Scary breathed real deep.

"And let's see, you take a ballet class, too, huh?" he said. "And gee, what a coincidence . . . on Saturday your teacher said you danced like a—"

"Gazill," I said very fast.

"Ga*zelle,*" said Mr. Scary.

"Whatever," I said.

My teacher sucked in his cheeks and looked at the paper again.

"And you were *punctual,* too," he said. "That's *amazing,* isn't it?"

I looked up at him.

"Well, you know . . . not if you get an early start," I said real soft.

Mr. Scary bent down next to me. His face was not jolly.

"Junie B. Jones, do you have *any* idea how disappointed I am in you right now?"

Just then, tears came in my eyes. And I didn't even expect that trouble.

I quick hanged my head so he couldn't see.

"Sorry," I said. "Sorry you're disappointed."

Mr. Scary took a big breath. He said we would talk more at recess.

Then he gave me a tissue from his pocket. And I wiped my tears.

After that, we went back into the room.

I sat down at my desk very slumping.

'Cause what do you know?

I didn't luck out after all.

# 4

# Cheater Pants

It's still dumb Monday

Dear first-grade journal,

Right now it is recess.

I am not playing on the playground.

~~Insted~~ Instead I am sitting at my desk. And I'm waiting to get yelled at.

I wish I could ~~disapeer~~ disappear into thin hair. If I could disappear,

I ~~woud~~ would run outside. And I ~~woud~~ would find May. And I ~~woud~~ would clunk her on the head.

I wish I didn't even sit next to that girl. 'Cause people should never leave homework on their desk for other people to borrow.

That is just asking for ~~truble~~ trouble, mister.

From,
Junie B., First Grader

Mr. Scary was writing at his desk.

He looked up and called my name.

"Junie B.?" he said. "I'm ready for you

now. Could you bring your chair up here, please?"

My stomach flipped and flopped. 'Cause here came the yelling part, that's why.

I did some deep breaths.

Then I pulled my chair to the front of the room. And I sat down next to him.

Mr. Scary took my homework paper out of his drawer. He set it in front of me very serious.

"I want you to explain this, Junie B.," he said. "I want you to tell me exactly why you copied May's homework this morning."

I tried to swallow, but nothing went down.

"Um, well, let's see . . . the reason I copied was . . . was . . ."

I tapped on my chin.

Then, all of a sudden . . . I thought of it!

"Daddy!" I said. "It was my daddy's fault!"

My teacher looked surprised at that answer.

"Your daddy?" he said. "Your *daddy* told you to copy May's homework?"

"Yes," I said. "I mean, no. I mean, last night I wanted to stay up late to do my homework. But Daddy turned out my light. And so he is the reason that I had to come to school without it."

"Ohhhh . . . *I* see," said my teacher. "Your daddy wouldn't let you stay up. So *that's* what forced you to copy May's paper."

I nodded real fast. "Yes," I said. "That's exactly it."

Mr. Scary raised his eyebrows. "So did

May actually *give* you her paper to copy?" he asked next.

I rolled my eyes at that crazy question.

"No, silly. May would never be *that* nice," I said. "It's just that this morning she kept on bragging about how her homework is always an A+. And then she left the paper on top of her desk when she went to the office. And that is just *asking* for trouble, mister."

Mr. Scary leaned back in his chair.

"Ah," he said. "So when May left for the office, you saw her paper and you just decided to—"

"*Borrow* it," I said. "I decided to borrow it to copy."

My teacher did a frown. "*Borrow?*" he said. "No, Junie B. I'm sorry. But *borrow* is not the right word here at all. When you copy someone else's paper, that's called *cheating.*"

My eyes got big and shocked at that word. 'Cause what was he even talking about?

"*No,* Mr. Scary. *No.* I didn't cheat. I didn't," I said. "Cheating is when you steal answers off of someone's *test.* But homework isn't a test. Homework doesn't even count, hardly."

"Oh, but homework *does* count, Junie B.," he said back. "Cheating is not just about stealing *test* answers. Cheating is anytime you take someone else's work and you present it as your own."

He looked at me.

"When you cheated this morning, you broke my trust in you, Junie B.," he said. "We have a rule about this in Room One.

We keep our eyes on our own papers. You've heard me say that a hundred times, I bet."

I felt surprised at that information.

"That's a rule?" I said. "No kidding? I always thought that was . . . well, you know . . . just a *suggestion.*"

Mr. Scary rolled his eyes. "No, Junie B. It's not a suggestion. It's definitely a rule," he said. "And it's an important rule, too."

I drummed my fingers on the desk.

"Well, I'll be darned," I said.

After a while, I did a deep breath.

"I'm sorry," I said real soft.

Mr. Scary smiled a little bit. "I'm sorry, too, Junie B.," he said. "But at least now I think we understand each other better. I will not put up with cheaters in my classroom."

I did a wince. "Yeah, only I wish you wouldn't keep saying that *cheater* word," I said. "'Cause I didn't even know I was cheating, hardly. Plus I don't like cheaters, either, Mr. Scary. On account of my daddy cheated me at Old Maid last week. And I am still not over that terrible experience."

Mr. Scary wrinkled his eyebrows. "Your daddy cheated?" he said.

I did a sigh. "Yes," I said. "Daddy raised the Old Maid way high in his hand so I would pick her. And then I did. And so what kind of sneaky trick was that?"

Mr. Scary covered his mouth.

He was shocked, I believe.

I leaned closer to him. "And Daddy is not the *only* cheater pants in my family, either," I said very quiet. "On account of my grampa Frank Miller is supposed to be on a diet. But yesterday, my grandma found an empty pie pan in his closet. And all that was left was a little bit of crust and a plastic fork."

I thought for a second. "No wonder I cheated," I said. "Cheating is in my blood, apparently."

Mr. Scary did a chuckle. "Well, nobody's perfect," he said. "Everyone cheats on a diet once in a while, I think. But cheating at school is a *very* different matter, Junie B. Cheating in school is serious business. Are we clear on that now?"

I nodded real fast. "Clear," I said.

After that, both of us shook hands. And Mr. Scary carried my chair back to my desk.

After I sat down, he took an envelope out of his pocket. And he handed it to me.

"I wrote a note to your parents explaining what happened this morning," he said. "I would like them to read it and sign it, okay? You can bring it back to me in the morning."

I did a gasp at that thing.

"No, Mr. Scary. *Not* okay," I said. "Please, don't make me take a note home. Please. I really, really don't want to take a note."

Mr. Scary thought for a second. Then he took the note back.

"Well, okay," he said. "If you feel that strongly, I won't make you take it."

He started walking back to his desk.

"I'll just call them tonight instead," he said.

I did a loud groan. 'Cause what kind of dumb choice is *that*?

I stomped to his desk and I grabbed back the note.

Then I stuffed it into my backpack.

And I sat down at my desk.

And I wrote in my journal one more time.

MR. SCARY IS A TATTLETALE!

# 5

# The Note

That night at dinner, I couldn't swallow my meatball. 'Cause how can you swallow a meatball when there's a note from your teacher in your pocket?

Mother kept on looking at my plate.

"What's the trouble with you tonight, honey?" she asked. "You love spaghetti and meatballs."

I picked up my fork real slow.

Then I put it right down again.

"Is something wrong, Junie B.?" asked Daddy. "Are you sick?"

I got down from my chair. And I stood by the table.

Then I hanged my head. And very slow, I took the note out of my pocket.

"I did something bad at school today," I said real glum. "And so there's something I have to give you."

I rocked back and forth on my feet for a minute.

Then I quick threw the note on the table.

And I ran to my room as fast as I could!

I shut the door real hard.

Then I ran around and around in circles. 'Cause I didn't actually have a plan, that's why.

My stuffed animals looked shocked at me.

*What's wrong, Junie B.?* said my

Raggedy Ann named Ruth. *Are you in trouble?*

*Of course she's in trouble,* said my Raggedy Andy named Larry. *Can't you tell? I bet Mother and Daddy are going to be running in here any second.*

My elephant named Philip Johnny Bob did fast thinking.

*Hide, Junie B.!* he told me. *Hide in the closet until they calm theirselves down.*

I nodded at that good idea.

Elephants are the smartest stuffed animals there is.

After that, I quick grabbed him by his foot. And we ran into my closet.

We climbed over shoes and games. Then we scrunched way down in the corner.

Pretty soon, we heard Mother and Daddy come in my room.

Our hearts started to pound and pound.

Then we tried to scrunch even smaller. Only too bad for us. Because Philip Johnny

Bob accidentally knocked over a shoe box. And it made a loud crashing sound.

Mother and Daddy opened the closet door.

I waved at them real pleasant.

"Hello. How are you today?" I said.

Philip Johnny Bob held out his arms.

*I love you people,* he said.

Daddy rolled his eyes.

Then he came into the closet. And he carried us out.

He sat me and Philip Johnny Bob on my bed.

Mother sat next to us. "You didn't have to hide from us, Junie B.," she said. "Daddy and I didn't come to yell at you. We just came in to talk about this."

I flopped back on my bed. And I put my pillow on my head.

"Yeah, only I already *did* talk about this, Mother," I said real muffly. "Me and Mr. Scary talked about this for a jillion million hours at recess."

Mother took the pillow off my head.

"Yes, I'm sure you did," she said. "But Daddy and I need to talk to you, too, Junie B. Copying someone else's work is a *very* serious matter, honey."

Daddy nodded. "Cheating is wrong," he said. "We want to make sure you understand that."

I did a big breath at that man.

"But I already *do* understand that, Daddy," I said. "I don't even like cheaters myself."

I thought for a minute. Then, all of a sudden, I remembered about the Old Maid.

I sat right up. "And anyway, if you think

cheating is so wrong, then how come you do it yourself?" I said. "Huh, Daddy? Huh?"

Daddy looked shocked at me.

"What?" he said. "What are you talking about? I don't cheat."

"Yes, you do *too* cheat," I said back. "On account of last week you cheated me at Old Maid. And I am still not over that terrible experience."

"Junie B., that's *not* true," Daddy said. "I already explained that to you, remember? When you raise the Old Maid above the other cards in your hand, it's not cheating. It's part of the fun."

"Yeah, only it *wasn't* fun," I said. "It wasn't! 'Cause after you raised her up there, you did a wink at me . . . like it wasn't really her. Only it WAS her, Daddy! And so what kind of sneaky trick was that?"

Daddy rolled his eyes way up at the ceiling. Then he shook his head kind of annoyed. And he left my room.

Mother ruffled my hair. "Sorry, honey," she said. "But I'm afraid Daddy is right on this one. What he did was sneaky, but it wasn't cheating. Trying to fool the other person is supposed to be part of the game."

After that, she went to go start my bath water.

Me and Philip Johnny Bob flopped back on my pillow.

We did a sigh.

'Cause grown-ups never do anything wrong, it seems.

Not even when they do.

# 6

# Tin Can

The next morning, I sat next to Herb on the bus. I sit next to him every single day. On account of that's what bestest friends automatically do.

Herb started talking about his new dog, Dilly. Only I couldn't even pay attention that good. 'Cause how can you talk about Dilly when you've still got a note from your teacher in your pocket?

Mother and Daddy had signed that dumb thing. And now I had to take it back to Mr. Scary.

I slumped way down in my seat. School was not being fun these days.

I looked at Herb.

I wished I could tell him about my problem. Only what if he didn't like cheaters? And he found out I *was* one? And then he didn't like me, either?

I thought and thought real hard.

Then finally, I took a deep breath. And I decided to risk it.

I leaned real close to his ear. And I whispered to him very secret.

"Okay. Here's the situation, Herb," I said. "I'm in a little bit of trouble at school. Only I'm really not bad. I promise. It's just that yesterday I accidentally did something wrong. But I don't actually want to tell you what it was . . . or else you might not like me anymore."

Herb looked at me and shrugged. "You copied May's homework when she went to the office," he said.

I did a gasp at that boy.

Because how did he know that private information?

I scratched my head. "But . . . but . . . how did you even—"

Herb interrupted me. "I saw you," he said. "Lennie and José saw you, too. You're a terrible sneak, Junie B. *Really* terrible, I mean."

I did a little frown.

That was not a compliment, possibly.

Herb patted my arm. "Don't worry. We still like you," he said. "Just don't copy May's homework anymore. And then you won't get in any more trouble."

I nodded my head.

Then I patted him back.

That Herb is good for me, I think.

Me and Herbert walked to Room One together.

Then we stopped right in our footsteps!

Because wowie wow wow!

That whole room looked different, I tell you!

Instead of being in rows, all of the desks were arranged in groups of circles!

We looked in the back to where we sit. There were five desks in our group.

May was already in her seat.

She was cleaning her desktop with a moist towelette.

Just then, Lennie and José walked in behind us.

"Whoa!" said Lennie.

"What's going on here?" said José.

Mr. Scary told us to please find our desks. And he will explain this in a minute.

All of us went back and sat down.

Sitting in a circle feels friendly.

We waved and smiled at each other.

Only not May.

She looked smuggy at us.

"I already know why we're sitting like this," she said. "I was the first one here this morning. And when you're first, you get to *know* stuff."

José stared at her moist towelette. He made the cuckoo sign.

Just then, Mr. Scary went to the board. And he wrote a weird word.

"Boys and girls, this morning we're going to be doing a poetry assignment," he said. "That's why I arranged your desks like this. I want you to be able to talk over your thoughts and share ideas."

He pointed at the weird word.

It was spelled c-i-n-q-u-a-i-n.

"Does anyone want to try and pronounce this?" he asked. "Hmm? Does anyone want to sound it out?"

May jumped right up.

*"Tin can!"* she shouted. "It's pronounced *tin can*!"

She grinned real delighted. "I know it's *tin can* because you told me that this morning, remember? I was the first one here. And I saw you write it on the board. And you told me it was pronounced *tin can*!"

Mr. Scary looked puzzled at her.

"Gee, I'm sorry, May. But it's not *tin can,*" he said. "You must not have heard me correctly. This word is pronounced like the words *sin* and *cane*. Sin-cane."

May crossed her arms.

"No," she said. "I'm sure that's not what you told me. You said it was *tin can,* Mr. Scary. You know you did."

Mr. Scary frowned. "No, May. I *didn't,*" he said. "Now please take your seat."

May sat down in a huff. She put her head on her desk and hid under her sweater.

Mr. Scary looked back to the board.

"A *cinquain* is a poem that has five lines," he said. "And each line has its own special rule."

He wrote the five rules.

***1st line:*** *One word (title)*

***2nd line:*** *Two words that describe the title*

***3rd line:*** *Three action words about the title*

***4th line:*** *Four words that express a thought or feeling about the title*

***5th line:*** *One word that means the same thing as the title*

After that, he wrote a cinquain for us to see. It was a poem called "Pickle."

*Pickle.*
*Bumpy, lumpy,*
*Crunching, munching, lunching,*
*Cucumbers makin' you pucker,*
*Gherkin.*

I laughed at that crazy thing. 'Cause whoever heard of a pickle poem?

"Writing a cinquain is fun," I said. "This assignment will be a breeze, I think."

Mr. Scary smiled. "Well, sometimes poems come very easily, Junie B. And other times they don't. But if you share words and ideas with each other, you can really help spark your imaginations," he said.

He looked all around. "In fact, I thought it might be fun for some of you to write your poem as a team," he said.

May quick came out from under her sweater at that news.

She looked at our group.

"Okay. Fine. I'll be the team leader," she told us.

After that, she made a mean face at Mr. Scary. And she took out her pencil.

"I know just what we're going to write about, too," she said kind of growly.

She waved her hands at us. "You four guys just talk about your normal stupid stuff, and I'll write the poem," she said. "I'll read it to you when I get done."

Lennie looked disappointed. "But Mr. Scary said we should write our poem *together,* May," he said.

"Sí," said José. "We're supposed to share thoughts and ideas, remember?"

May threw her hands in the air.

"I *knew* it!" she said. "I knew working as a team wouldn't work. Fine. You guys just write your own dumb poem. And I'll write mine."

After that, she took her pencil and paper. And she hid under her sweater again.

All of us looked at each other and

shrugged. Then we started right to work.

I tapped on my chin.

"Hmm. It says the first line needs to be the title," I said. "So maybe the title should come first."

May peeked her eyes out at me. "Duh," she said.

José covered her up again.

Just then, Herb raised his hand.

"Hey! I know," he said. "Since Mr. Scary wrote a pickle poem, why don't we write one about an olive?"

He leaned back in his chair and did a happy thumbs-up.

No one did a thumbs-up back.

'Cause what kind of dumb idea was that?

"An olive?" I said.

"I hate olives," said José.

"I threw up an olive once," said Lennie.

Herb looked irritated at us.

I patted him. "Don't be mad," I said. "It's just that maybe there's something funner to write about than an olive, that's all."

"Sí," said José. "Like maybe we could write about soccer. Playing soccer is fun, right?"

"Yes," I said. "Plus riding the bus to school is fun, too. Right, Herb? Me and you always have fun on the bus. Don't we?"

Lennie shook his head. "But I don't ride the bus, Junie B.," he said. "I think we should write about something that *all* of us know about."

He thought for a second. Then he clapped his hands together.

"I know! We could write about how all of us shampoo our hair to keep it healthy and shiny! All of us do that, right?"

After that, me and José and Herb just looked and looked at him.

'Cause sometimes Lennie is off the deep end, that's why.

Finally, José put his head on his desk.

"Maybe we're making this too hard," he said. "Why can't we just write about something easy? Like about how all of us are friends or something."

Herb smiled a little bit. "Yeah. That's a good idea. We could write about the four of us. And we could call it 'Friends.'"

José smiled, too. "Sí," he said. "Or 'Amigos,' maybe."

Just then, I bounced up and down real excited.

'Cause the perfect title just hit me, that's why! It hit me right out of the clear blue sky!

"PALLIES!" I said. "Let's call it 'Pallies'! 'Cause that's what we are, right? All four of us are bestest *pallies*! And 'Pallies' sounds like a cute title, don't you think?"

I looked at them real hopeful.

Then all of my pallies started to smile.

Our poem was off to a great start!

# 7

# Pallies

We worked on our poems for the whole entire morning, almost.

And ha! Mr. Scary was right! Sharing ideas *did* help spark our imaginations! Plus all of us got to add our own special words to our poem! And that is called good teamwork!

After we got done, I printed our poem on a clean piece of paper.

Lennie and José and Herb watched me real careful.

"I am an excellent printer," I told them.

"I can print with the best of them."

Pretty soon, all of the other children in Room One finished their poems, too.

And good news! Mr. Scary said there was time to read some of our poems to the class.

Lucille didn't wait to get called on.

She ran right to the front of the room. And she made squinty eyes at Camille and Chenille.

"I wanted to write my poem with two girls in my group," she said. "But all they wanted to write about was twins, twins, twins."

She looked at them some more.

"The whole world is not just about you two, you know," she grouched.

After that, she fluffed her lacy dress. And she read her poem:

*Me.*
*Richie Lucille.*
*Shopping, buying, spending.*
*Everyone's jealous of myself.*
*Princess.*

After she was finished, Mr. Scary sat there for a second.

Then he smiled and nodded.

"Good, Lucille. Yes. Excellent," he said. "That poem really says it all, doesn't it?"

Lucille nodded. "Yes," she said. "It does."

Then she did another mean look at the twins. And she sat back down.

After that, May didn't wait to be called on, either. She ran to the front of the room just like Lucille. And she hollered out her poem real loud.

*Tin Can!*
*Tin-tin, Can-can!*
*I have perfect hearing!*
*And Mr. Scary told me it was* tin can!
*He did, he did, he really did!*

Mr. Scary rubbed his chin.

"Yes, well, that certainly was an interesting poem idea, May. But it didn't really follow the rules of a cinquain, did it?" he said.

"You mean *tin can,*" said May.

Mr. Scary did a sigh.

Then he got up from his desk. And he walked May back to her seat.

After that, there was time for one more poem.

My group waved our hands all around in the air.

"We have a good one!" hollered José.

"Yes! A *really* good one!" yelled Lennie.

Mr. Scary nodded at us.

And so all of us jumped up. And we stood in our group. And we read our poem with all of our voices.

Pallies.
Chummy, happy,
Joking, gelling, sharing.
Four amigos all together.
Friendship.

# 8

# A+ Us

A+!

We got an A+ on our poem!

Mr. Scary came right back to our desks.

And he took his red pencil.

And he wrote an A+ right on top of our paper!

"What a *wonderful* poem you guys wrote," he said. "I loved that."

We jumped and clapped for ourselves.

It was the funnest morning I ever saw.

And that is not all! 'Cause lunch and recess kept on being fun, too. On account of when four friends are in happy moods together, life is a joy, I tell you!

After recess, I hurried back to Room One. 'Cause I couldn't wait to see what happy assignment we would do next.

I skipped in the room and looked at the board.

And then, boom!

I came to a screechy stop.

On account of the board had two terrible words on it!

It said, SPELLING TEST!

And I forgot all about that stupid thing!

That dumb test was supposed to be last Friday. And then it got put off till today. And so how was I even supposed to remember that last night? 'Cause I was worried about my note, of course.

My legs felt weakish and limpish.

Very slow, I dragged my feet back to my seat.

The desks were back to normal again.

Herb was already sitting down. He turned around and looked at me.

"What's wrong, Junie B.?" he asked. "Don't you feel good?"

I laid my head on my desk.

"I forgot to study my spelling words last night," I said. "And now I'm going to be in trouble with Mother and Daddy again."

I did a whine. "This is the whole dumb problem with school," I said. "One minute you're all joyful and happy. And the next minute, the joy gets flushed right out of you."

Herb tried to make me feel better.

"Don't worry. Most of the words are easy this week," he said.

He paused for a second. "Sort of."

I did another whine. 'Cause *sort of* does not mean "really."

In the front of the room, Mr. Scary was passing out paper.

"Is everybody ready for our spelling test this week?" he said.

He winked. "Since you had four extra nights to study, I'm sure everyone will get a perfect grade, right?"

My stomach turned into a knotball at that comment.

Pretty soon, the test began.

Mr. Scary pronounced the first spelling word. And he used it in a sentence.

*"Fox,"* he said. "The *fox* is running through the woods. *Fox*."

I perked up a little bit. 'Cause I know how to spell *fox,* of course.

I printed it very neat on my paper.

fox

"The next word is *box,*" said Mr. Scary. "I keep all my toys in a *box*. *Box*."

I sat up even perkier. Because ha! *Box* is just as easy as *fox*!

box

Mr. Scary smiled. "The next word is *would,*" he said. "I *would* like all of you to do well on this test. *Would.*"

Just then, I stopped perking. 'Cause sometimes I get mixed up on that one.

I wrote down some letters.

wood

Then I crossed them out. On account of that was the wrong kind of wood, I believe.

I tried again.

woud

~~wood~~

I shook my head. That didn't look right, either.

Finally, I covered my face and I did a groan.

"Shh!" said May.

Herb started to turn around to see what was the matter. Then he quick stopped himself. 'Cause no turning around during a test, of course.

I looked at what I wrote some more. Then I strained my brain to try and remember how to spell it. Only nothing came to me.

Finally, I did another groan.

And *that's* when a miracle happened!

My friend Herbert came to my rescue!

First, he shifted a teensy bit in his chair. Then he moved his test paper to where I could see it. And he pointed to the word with his finger.

My mouth came open at that lovely gesture.

'Cause I didn't even ask him to do that! Herb just *gave* that word to me.

Like a gift!

I stretched my neck to see it better.

And yay! As soon as I saw the word, my imagination got sparked! And I remembered the letter *l* perfectly good!

I quick wrote it down on my paper.

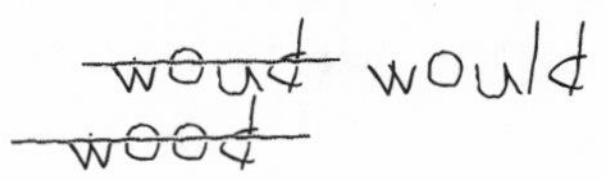


I was just in time!

Mr. Scary was already on the next word.

"*Peek,*" he said. "I saw you *peek. Peek.*"

Just then, I sat in my seat very still. And I did a gulp. 'Cause I really thought he saw me *peek,* that's why.

Only good news! I was wrong!

On account of he *didn't* see me peek. He *didn't*! And besides, what I did this time wasn't even bad, probably. Because Herb *shared* that word with me. Just like we shared words for our poem.

Finally, I did a little sigh. And I wrote *peek* on my paper.

After that, I took the rest of the spelling test very perfect.

And I put what happened right out of my brain.

Sort of.

# 9

# Sleeping on It

That night, me and Philip Johnny Bob didn't sleep that good.

We tossed and turned a real lot.

Also, Philip Johnny Bob talked in his sleep a little bit. 'Cause I heard him say the word *cheater pants*.

I woke him up when I heard that. Then both of us got a drink of water. And we talked about what was the trouble.

The next morning, our eyes were poopish and droopy.

And guess what? We were not the only

ones who looked like that, either. 'Cause when my friend Herb got on the bus, his eyes were poopish and droopy, too.

He plopped down next to me. And he did a big yawn.

"I didn't sleep good last night," he said real tired.

I nodded. "Me too, Herb. I didn't sleep good, too," I said.

Herb sat there a minute. Then he did a sigh.

"Yeah, only I don't even want to tell you *why* I didn't sleep," he said. "Or maybe you might get mad at me."

I raised my eyebrows at him. "Oh?"

Herb squirmed in his seat kind of uncomfortable. Then he quieted his voice.

"It's kind of about the spelling test," he whispered.

I thought about that. "Oh," I said. "Oh, yeah. I guess I didn't thank you for helping me, did I?"

I patted his arm.

"Thank you, Herb," I said. "Because of

you, I will always remember how to spell the word *would*."

Herb's shoulders slumped way down.

"Yeah, see . . . but *that's* the problem, Junie B.," he said. "*That's* why I didn't sleep last night. Because I'm sorry, but I don't feel that good about helping you."

He squirmed some more.

"I mean, at the time, I thought it would be nice. But as soon as I showed you my test, it didn't feel nice at all. Instead, it felt like . . . well, you know, it felt like I was a—"

I quick sat up and interrupted him.

"A *cheater pants*!" I said. "It felt like you were a cheater pants. Right, Herb? Right? *That's* how come you couldn't sleep last night, correct? 'Cause at first you thought it would be nice to share with me.

Only as soon as you did it, it felt kind of wrong inside."

Herb looked surprised at me. "Yeah, it did. But how did you even *know* that?"

"*Because,* Herb. *Because,*" I said. "Have you forgotten who you are talking to here? I am a cheater pants myself, remember? So I know exactly what it feels like!"

I shook my head.

"I can't believe it, Herb. I can't believe I did it two days in a row," I said. "'Cause on Monday I copied May's homework. And yesterday I copied your spelling word. Only at first, I tried to pretend that you and me were just sharing."

Herb nodded kind of sad. "Yeah. But we weren't, were we?" he said.

"No," I said back. "We really weren't, Herbert. On account of sharing on a spelling test is called *cheating*."

Herbert did a wince at that word.

I patted him. "I know just how you feel, pally," I said. "The word *cheater* makes you feel like a nasty, rotten ratty pants who can't even be trusted."

Herb nodded. Then he smiled a little bit.

"You have a nice way with words," he said.

I did a shrug. "Actually, Philip Johnny Bob came up with that one."

After that, me and Herb rode the rest of the way to school without talking.

We both felt better, I think.

We told on ourselves at recess.

Me and Herbert.

Both of us.

Together.

We went to Room One after lunch. And we told Mr. Scary that we cheated on the spelling test.

Herb explained about how he heard me being upset during the test. And he didn't want me to get in trouble with Mother and Daddy again. So he showed me his answer so I would do good.

Then I explained about how that was a lovely gesture by Herbert. But after we did it, we both knew it was wrong. And so we will never, ever do that again. And we *mean* it.

Mr. Scary listened to us real careful.

Then he thanked us for our honesty. And he said he admired us very much for telling him what we did.

After that, he got out our test papers. And he wrote big zeros right at the top of them. On account of even if you get admired, you still get a zero, apparently.

Only that was not even the end of it.

Because that night—while I was eating dinner—Mr. Scary called my house. And he tattletaled to Mother right on the phone.

At first, Mother frowned a real, real lot.

Then me and her and Daddy talked about cheating all over again. And I got yelled at a little bit.

But later, when they tucked me into bed, they said they were proud of me and Herb for telling on ourselves. And all of us ended up hugging.

That night, Philip Johnny Bob and I slept very perfect.

Only here is the happiest news of *all.*

When me and Herb got to school the next day, Mr. Scary called us up to his desk. And he gave each of us a special poem that he wrote all by himself!

I tried to read mine, but I didn't know all the words. So Mr. Scary read it to me.

After he finished, I smiled real proud.

Then I read it one more time. To just myself.

*Junie (B.)*
*Bubbly, bouncy.*
*Learning, growing, glowing.*
*Your HONESTY is awesome!*
*Trusted.*

Barbara Park is one of today's funniest authors. Her Junie B. Jones books are consistently on the *New York Times* and *USA Today* bestseller lists. Her middle-grade novels, which include *Skinnybones, The Kid in the Red Jacket, Mick Harte Was Here,* and *The Graduation of Jake Moon,* have won over forty children's book awards. Barbara holds a B.S. in education. She has two grown sons and lives with her husband, Richard, in Arizona.

Denise Brunkus's entertaining illustrations have appeared in over fifty books. She lives in New Jersey with her husband and daughter.